BRAMBLES

VEE

To my wonderful parents, for all their love, support and encouragement. To my incredible friends, for their patience and willingness to pore over my drafts and half-finished works. To my sister, for her constant faith in my abilities. To my darling ***Raylla****, for bringing her light into the dark of my little world.*

And to the loathsome teacher(s) who made school a living hell- the only thing I gained under your tutelage was a capacity for spite so great, it pushed me to finish this book.

Cheers, we've finally made it!

Contents

Acknowledgements

First and foremost, I'd like to acknowledge the writer of this anthology; myself.

My absence would, I believe, hinder this process significantly.

I would dedicate this book to myself, but I have a queue of people all glaring over my shoulder, demanding that they be included, so this little note to myself will have to do.

Congratulations love, you've stuck it out.

Then, I would like to thank my mother for all the efforts she's put into making this brainchild of mine something more tangible. Without her guidance, I doubt this book would have been anything more than a pipe dream. So thankyou for that, mum!

Next, I'd like to thank my father for his unwavering support and encouragement. He never once let my dreams die, and that, I think, is the reason I made it to the halfway point.

Thirdly, my sister, for never once doubting me, and for providing me with a steady supply of new music and chocolate that helped me power through the tough times.

Fourthly, Sam, Jo and Ann, for always having my back and being my personal cheerleaders.

Lastly, I must once again give a shoutout to my beloved beagle for simply existing and letting me, for as long as I'm by her side, simply exist too.

Preface

In the depths of my mind there took root a place whose name I do not know, whose purpose is wholly unknown to me.

What lives on that plane of my creation? What unfolds when my eyes slide shut?

Stories.

Millions and millions of stories.

They played out in my head- synchronous, yet unaware of one another.

Sometimes, I give them more than their half-lives. I give them *meaning,* you see.

And now I want to whisper that meaning out into the world.

Who knows? Maybe you'll hear it too

1

The Terrible Ordeal Of Being

The Void lay nestled between her ribs, clasping the heart in a loving embrace.

The maddening thing about the Void was its ever changing desires.

Some days, the Void ached with the need for *more*. The Void would guzzle all that she could give and still demand that it be satiated.

The Void would hum and buzz and whir until she took notice and promised to satisfy its ever present gluttony.

But some nights, when the icy white expanse outside reflected in panicked pupils blown wide by worry, the Void wanted Nothing.

It wanted to be lost. Destroyed. *Massacred*.

It screamed and begged until she sobbed and drew blood with her nails, until she left scabs and untold stories on her arms and neck.

The Void was everything. The Void didn't exist. The Void pushed her forward. The Void dragged her down in a never-ending dance of death.

She was floating untethered. She was drowning; anchored and moored.

Sometimes the Void spared her, let her daydream wistfully about all that could never be.

Other days it was not so forgiving, reminding her of all that she *couldn't, wouldn't* or *didn't.*

The past, the present and the future all mashed together in a jarring blur. She felt as though she was looking through a foggy mirror. She felt as though she was looking through another's eyes.

The Void did all this and more.

It wrapped its fingers steadily around the heart's neck, it pressed possessive kisses to the mind, and it melded against the soul until she couldn't tell one apart from the other.

Her very own blackhole; unable to save itself and yet cutting away every last life line. She could only watch in mute horror as this terrible paradox played out over and over again.

For so long she had believed that being hollow was beautiful.

Birds' bones were hollow and it lifted them up into clear skies.

Tree trunks were hollow and they fostered and nourished the homes of the chipper squirrels and the hooting owls.

She had thought that being hollow left space for growing. For being slowly filled.

But she hadn't realised that hollow meant empty. She had never wondered how the hole felt before the last handful of dirt was patted down.

And now she knew. She knew and this knowledge enriched her not even one little bit.

This knowledge was a rusty knife; blunt and painful. Useless, but still able to wreak havoc.

Oh, what she would have given to rid herself of this plague! Of this *chasm* that paraded around in her skin.

She had no saviour. She had not even *herself.*

All that was left was the terrible, terrible *emptiness* - unyielding as smoke - and the flickering embers of her fast dying hope.

2

Ad Idem

"Isn't it enough?" Asked the Lady fair.

Fair, thought I, has two meanings; to be beautiful, and this woman was as lovely as the much praised Moon, and to be Just, and there was no one who teetered as precisely and perfectly as she on the scales of truth and righteousness.

"Nothing is enough for me", said I at last, my tongue much emboldened. Where we stood that fateful day no secrets were kept.

"I am your creator", said she, "I stoke the flame that burns in your belly. I widen the yawning void within your heart. Do not assume that I am unaware of your desires when it is my will that makes them so"

"I do not presume that we are equals", spoke I, trying to douse the passion that she was revered for, "but we both must acknowledge that I have no control in this realm. It is not mine, much as my mind is not mine"

"But your words are your own", observed she keenly, "that, I take no credit for, for this was always the case"

"I have found, my lady, that holding my tongue muted no one but me", said I, bitterness as clear as day.

"You changed the course", said the Lady with narrowed eyes, "of our scintillating conversation. You speak of yearning for more, and yet you have spent your time at a standstill"

"My time was mine to spend"

"But it was not yours to end", said She, and she turned her face away from me so that I mightn't look upon her sorrow.

"That, my Lady", said I, choosing my words carefully, "is not for either of us to say"

I expected castigation. I did not expect muffled cries.

"For you, I have given everything", she sobbed, "I have given you no path in hopes that you might make your own. You dug your way out of a hole that did not exist"

"You hoped that I would set a target but I remained aimless. I have no insight into your divine machinations. I didn't know what you expected of me, so I wished to find out that particular secret from its keeper"

"Then you have lost it all on a fool's errand", boomed the Lady, "for I am not the keeper of your secret. I am the wind that blows it along. I do not hold onto what is not mine, much like you do not hold onto what is yours"

"It was my choice to make", I repeat mulishly.

"And your consequences another must bear", she snarled, "you crack the glass and another must cut themselves open trying to fit together the shards"

"I did not wish to do what I did!", I burst out at last, "You, who gives life to all. You, who watches as we step where you direct us to and leap away from where you ask us to, you do not understand what it feels like to be but a puppet dangling from invisible strings"

"A *puppet*", she whispered in a grieved voice, "you, my precious creation, a puppet?"

"I was not living a life", I said, needing the world to hear that verity, "how could I have destroyed what never was whole?"

My Lady shed her tears then. She looked upon me and wept, and I looked on with glazed eyes at the last being grieving for what would never again be.

3

Musings Of The Supine

The librarian walked by mahogany alcoves, humming a song lost to time.

Many things were lost to time, she supposed; the failure of her predecessors no doubt. But she wouldn't repeat their mistakes. She was better than that.

The alcoves had maple shelves, stacked with volumes upon volumes upon volumes. She was noting a reoccurring theme in this particular archive; the Earth. Trees. Wood.

Some deep roots in this one.

Her gentle fingers were long and nimble and looked as though they should be plucking the strings of a harp, although their color was the fine ivory of another instrument's keys.

Those fingers brushed each tome's spine, her touch as soft as a feather light kiss.

The Librarian breathed, centering herself as all the memories and wisdom the book possessed flung into her mind.

So chaotic. But she would give it order...

She passed to the next volume and the next and the next until she finished an entire shelf's worth of stories.

Stories, she mused.

She liked that term. It fit what she saw.

The snippets and slideshows of a million minds all coming together in a beautiful starburst of images.

It made her reel with shock the first time, she remembered fondly.

How stupid she had been.

Excited too.

Her predecessor wasn't around, had faded into dust and shadows as she herself stepped into the light.

The odd transition hadn't hurt one bit. She couldn't remember much of anything, only a pleasant haze as she had mooned about that first decade or so.

Slowly, as her mind watched more and more lives unspool in her mind like a rolling ball of yarn, her own Self had faded.

Her family, if she had ever had one, had vanished in the wake of the smiles of one through another's eyes. Her beloved companions had disappeared, replaced by the loved ones of a million others.

Sometimes, she didn't recognize herself in the mirror.

How wan and wonder-filled she looked. Though, the two conflicting emotions seemed to fight for their place on her face every time.

She should cover the mirrors if they made her wax poetry about her appearance. She couldn't afford to indulge herself in such idle thoughts.

Really, wan and wonderfilled!

One would think she were the orator and not the voiceless audience.

Anyways, she had a job to do and that was all that mattered.

She firmly dismissed all her senseless, fantastical notions.

She was the Librarian, Keeper of Fables, not their maker.

But even so, as she walked past shelf after shelf, each filled to the brim, listening and hearing and knowing, she couldn't help but ask herself if anyone would ever tell her tale.

4

To Come Home

We have always existed in the empty spaces- just the two of us.

Some mornings are good; I remember first. Others are bad; he remembers.

But some- a few perfect golden sunrises- are the best; neither of us can recall.

On the rare occasion when that takes place, I wake up to iridescent light streaming in from the window, splaying across his face, turning flushed skin honey and warm.

Warm.

It's so warm in his embrace.

I don't want to move. I fear remembrance. Any sudden movement could jolt my memories. Or worse, his.

But I still get up. Like I always do.

I pad into the kitchen as softly as I can- barefoot, because I like to feel the tiles and jump across without touching the lines- and I begin inspecting the kitchen.

It feels like it's been forever since I've rummaged through these very same cupboards; brown with dull steel handles, worn and used and filled to the brim with cups, cutlery and a plethora of other things I can't remember.

Once I'd found a packet of batteries. He'd found my glasses in there too, on one of our frequent hunts after them (they always seemed to disappear when I needed them most)

I had memorized the tenderness with which he'd fit the glasses back onto my face, a quick press of his lips to my temple as he tucked back my hair.

I don't linger on that memory long. Reminiscing about one thing usually leads to a domino effect and I end up dredging up memories I've been trying to drown.

I root about for a bit before settling on a couple of fruits- bananas, apples and grapes- all fresh and sweet.

(He'd always had the sweet tooth of the two of us but I can still appreciate the rush of joy that comes from a particularly sugary treat)

I chop up the fruits, prepare a bowl of oatmeal as quickly as I can, and rush back to the room.

I don't want to miss even a second more of this glorious day.

I dive back under the covers.

"Good morning"

His voice is the same honey tone of his skin- rich and deep and warm.

"Your toes are all icy"

"I take back every nice thing I've said about you!"

I steal more of the covers but I cuddle closer to him. I think it's a fair trade.

"Who have you said nice things about me to?"

My heart sinks. One wrong word has always triggered my mind, memories rising unbidden and unwanted and unnecessary.

But I can't push them down. That is the one thing I'm not allowed in this world of dreams.

It's as though all my joy had been condensed into a beautiful little bubble, and now the bubble's been popped.

Sorrow rests in his eyes.

I never want to see that look again. I'd rip the world apart with my bare hands if it means keeping that expression off his face.

So hopeless. So *desolate.*

I wish I could tell him what he's feeling is only a fraction of what I'm going through.

"You have to go now, don't you?" He asks me, and if I hadn't spent years perfecting my poker face, I would have wept in his arms at the sadness in his voice.

"I don't want to"

"No?" He hums, like it's a question.

Like he doesn't know the answer.

Like he doesn't know what I'd give to be with him again.

(*Everything. I'd give everything*)

"No"

But it's too late. Already his face- carved into my mind by love and agony in equal measure- is fading, slowly but surely.

I would rather brand it in my heart permanently than forget, even if it's temporarily.

"Will you come back?"

No part of my heart is whole. But when he asks me that, the cracks seem more defined.

"To you? Always"

And then the unthinkable happens for the millionth time;

I wake up.

5

Find Solace

The Sun and the Moon in their infinite wisdom each appointed a guardian for themselves when the Earth first came to be.

The Sun elected the Dove, whose wings were as white as the snow its master's fire melted, and whose radiance shone above all that lived.

The Moon adopted the Crow, whose feathers ushered in a soft blanket of darkness and whose gentle gaze helped soothe the fears of all who looked to it for comfort.

For eons the two coexisted in peace and harmony, each bringing about their respective phenomena.

But the Dove soon grew jealous of the Crow, for it could hear the praise the Earth dwellers dispensed when night fell.

The Dove was a tough master- hard to please and quick to anger- and the earth dwellers had displeased it greatly with their affection for the Crow.

With a cacophonic trill, the Dove spread its wings and let the fury of the sun scorch the earth, blighting and smiting until the earth dwellers begged for forgiveness.

The Dove was smug and full of glee until it learnt that it had only succeeded in turning away it's worshippers. So it decided to take a different approach.

Every time it let gentle light filter onto the Earth it would whisper in the ears of all those who basked in it and poisoned their minds, telling them about the fearsome creatures lurking in the dark the Crow so favoured.

By and by, the earth dwellers turned against the Moon's chosen guardian. But the Crow still did its best, for its heart was free of the malice the earth dwellers now bore.

But by and by, the Crow grew tired of the suspicious glances and the fearful shouts the earthlings let out when it dropped its wings and welcomed in the night.

For decades it would suffer in silence until at last it could take it no more.

For years it had heard about its own supposedly grotesque nature, and it was more than willing to become the monster they had made it into.

But almost instantly after this thought struck it, it was filled with shame. How could it become as terrible as those who scorned it? How could it sink low enough to punish those who had never wronged?

So it fled from the skies and crept up to its mistress. It wept at her feet, narrating all the accusations and curses it had borne with grace and dignity- but no more. It could no longer serve those who hated and feared it so.

The Moon, on hearing her beloved guardian's heart-wrenching sobs, wept along, for didn't she too know what it felt like to dim in the presence of one more radiant and far more wrathful?

But as the Moon wept, her tears of compassion would fall to the ground- silvery and incandescent.

Where the droplets fell, the life was blessed with a gift.

They could see the beauty in the Crow as she had once done, hear the stories of the twinkling stars as she could, watch the shadows' shapes and marvel, feel a thrill of joy in the lonesomeness she brought and look up at the night sky in awe.

This gift would pass from creature to creature, letting them see the world for what it was and love it still, and the Crow rejoiced and spread its wings over the Earth once more.

Fin.

The strange thing about time and stories is that they're supposed to be infinite, and yet, us mortals seem to be in short supply of both.

I hope that someday, I can change at least one part of that paragraph.

9 798886 841596

Printed by Libri Plureos GmbH in Hamburg,
Germany